# THE
# PIANO

# THE PIANO

Edgar J. Hyde

**CCP**

© 1998 Children's Choice Publications Ltd

First printed 1998, reprinted 1998, reprinted 1999
Creepers and Edgar J. Hyde are registered Trademarks of
Children's Choice Publications Ltd.

Text supplied by Joan Love

ISBN 1-90201-207-0

Printed and bound in the UK

# Contents

# Chapter 1

Roger Houston checked his mirror, indicated left and drew the car to a halt by the side of the road. His wife, beside him, yawned and stretched.

"Where are we?" she asked sleepily.

"Somewhere known as Cramlington – isn't it quaint?" he replied. "I think I may fall asleep at the wheel if I don't get out for a while and stretch my legs. We'd better wake the children."

The Houston family were returning from their annual Easter holiday and had been driving since early that morning. Mr Houston felt his eyes ache with the strain of driving for so long and felt the need of some refreshment.

"Cramlington," thought Mr Houston, "looks like the perfect place to stop and have lunch."

The children, roused from sleep by their mother, were rubbing at their eyes, stretching wearily and making ready to get out of the car.

"Remember your cardigan, Victoria, it's probably colder than you think," said Mum. "You too, Darryn, where's your jacket gone?"

Mrs Houston fussed around getting the children ready while her husband leaned against the outside of the car, enjoying the fresh sea air.

"Nice place, this – really picturesque," he said to no-one in particular. "Strange we've never happened upon it before."

His thoughts were interrupted by his family spilling noisily out onto the pavement. Darryn's hair, as it was wont to do, stuck up in all different directions, while he could see his practically-a-teenager daughter check her reflection in the car's wing mirror, and smooth down her hair before making sure her metallic blue nail varnish was unchipped.

"Dad, Mum, can we go to the toy shop? Can we, please, please?" Darryn bounced up and down, looking eagerly from one to the other as he waited for his parents to answer. Dad shook his head sternly.

"Listen, young lad," he told his 6-year-old son, "we have enough new toys packed into the boot of the car without buying any more. I'm surprised the car was able to move at all with all that weight in the back."

Darryn looked momentarily crestfallen then, brightening, took his Dad's hand and asked "Can I buy some sweets then, Dad, can I please, I've got £2 left in my pocket, please."

Taking hold of his son's small, sticky hand ("What has that child been eating now?" he thought to himself), Dad turned left into a small side street before muttering absentmindedly, "Depends on whether or not you eat your lunch, my boy."

Mum and Victoria walked behind more leisurely – Mum admiring the pretty window boxes adorning the fronts of the small white-washed houses, Victoria looking hopefully for a sports or beauty shop. As they turned into the side street, they found Dad and Darryn, noses pressed hard against a shop window. Looking upwards, Mum noticed the sign "Larkspur Music" above the shop. She and her daughter joined the others, and they too pressed their noses against the window to view the instruments stored inside. Though everything looked pretty dusty, the family were thrilled to see a range of musical instruments; a cello, some violins, guitars, a huge drum kit which took up most of the left hand side of the window and lots more besides.

"Oh, do let's go in" Mum said, glancing at the "open" sign on the front of the door. Though neither she nor her husband had any musical skills to speak of, Emily Houston had always wanted to be able to play so*mething*. Pushing open the door, the family entered the shop and there, right in the centre, stood the most beautiful piano they had ever set eyes upon. Predominantly white, it stood proudly with its lid open, showing polished keys which seemed to simply cry out for someone to touch them. Victoria, three years into piano lessons, was the first to run her fingers along the keys.

"Oh Mum, Dad, it's perfect – can we buy it, please?"

Dad was aghast.

"Buy it, Victoria? You can't be serious –

do you know how much these things cost? Put the lid down, quickly, you're not supposed to touch, you know."

"Don't be so hard on her, dear," Mum intervened. "I can quite understand how she feels – it really is quite beautiful."

And she too moved closer to the piano and ran her own fingers along the keys. As a child, Emily Houston had hoped her parents would send her to piano lessons, but unfortunately the money was always needed elsewhere, and she had never fulfilled her wish.

"Can I help you?" came a voice from the far end of the shop. An elderly man was walking towards them. "Ah, you've taken a liking to the piano, have you my dear?" he smiled at Victoria.

"Well, yes, it is rather beautiful" she said. "I didn't mean to touch it, really, I just couldn't help myself."

"Oh, don't worry about that" he returned.

# Chapter 1

"Most people who come in here are drawn to the piano. Have a seat – what about you, young man? Would you like to sit on the stool alongside your sister?"

Darryn was seated on the stool almost before the words had left the shop owner's mouth. His sister, seated half-on and half-off, grimaced at her brother before gently touching the keys while Darryn, more brash than Victoria, began to roughly play his scales.

"Would you be interested in buying, Sir, Madam?" the man smiled at them both. "I'm quite sure you'll be surprised at the price."

Dad was in no doubt about that whatsoever!

"£200" the owner was saying. "And we'll deliver it for you, free of charge."

Dad smiled. The old guy must be under the impression they want to buy the *stool*!

"Now what on earth would be the point in having a stool with no pia—?"

His wife interrupted him.

"£200?" she turned quizzically to the man. "Does that include the stool, then?"

Though disbelieving of the price, she wasn't one to waste an opportunity!

"Yes, of course, madam. The piano, the stool and delivery. We can get it to you by, say, Monday morning." Checking the wall calendar quickly, he nodded his confirmation. "Yes, Monday should be fine. Now, if you'd just care to give me details of your address, we'll get the form filling done. Tedious, all the forms you have to complete these days."

And it was thus that the piano happened to belong to the Houston family. Dad left the shop in a complete daze, having filled in and signed a cheque for £200, given name, address, post code and telephone number to the shop owner, and stuffed a bill of sale in his wallet.

"Oh don't look like that, Roger," said

Mum. "It's such a stroke of luck, finding an instrument in that condition, and at that price."

Taking both her children by the hand, she strode off in front of her husband, leaving him to shake his head over the events which had just taken place.

# Chapter 2

"Here comes a van now!" shouted Darryn from upstairs.

He had been keeping watch since 8 am that morning, desperate for delivery of the piano, and now could hardly contain himself. Throwing himself down the stairs, he was first to the front door, almost tripping over a stray rollerblade in his haste.

The van drew up outside No. 21 and two men got out, made their way to the back of the van and unlocked the doors. Dad by now had appeared outside, and he directed the men to put the piano into the large room which was used partially for storage and partially for the children's toys. Everything in the room had been frantically pushed to one side that morning in order to make room for the family's new possession. Dad paid the men, thanked them graciously and shut the door, shaking his head disbelievingly, for he had truly never believed the family would ever see the piano again.

"Let me sit down, let me sit down!" shouted Darryn, as both children tried to push themselves onto the piano stool.

"It's not big enough for both of us," his older sister replied. "Get off – it's my turn first – you can't even play properly."

"Now, now," Mum intervened, "no fighting. What we'll do is have one hour for Victoria followed by one hour for Darryn. Victoria first, Darryn, come over here beside me and let your sister play."

Turning to her daughter, she continued

"And since you know an awful lot more about the piano than Darryn does, why don't you try and help him. Let's be constructive instead of bickering with one another."

Victoria shrugged non-noncommittally and turned her full attention to the gleaming keys, while Darryn stared at the clock, willing the next hour to pass quickly. And so the day passed, with both parents being aware of scales being practised, catching the odd snatch of "Chopsticks", intermingled with the children having the odd scuffle. At the end of the night everyone climbed wearily into bed and fell fast asleep.

Dad was the first one to wake the next morning. He looked at his alarm clockclock – 7.30! He nudged his wife.

"Emily? Do you hear that?"

Reluctantly she turned to face him.

"What is it dear? I'm sleepy." Then, realising her husband was sitting up in bed, she rubbed her eyes and sat up too. It was only then that she became aware of the strange and beautiful music drifting upstairs.

"Listen?" said her husband. "Can you hear it now? Come on, let's go downstairs – I didn't realise Victoria was quite so accomplished."

Mum and Dad both made their way to the top of the stairs and began their descent. The music still played, a haunting melody which neither seemed to have heard before. They went down the stairs quietly, not wanting to disturb Victoria, and somehow unwilling to cut into the perfection of the music. As they reached the last stair and rounded the hallway leading to the room which housed the piano, Dad stopped and gasped. For he could see, in the far corner of the room, not touching the piano, Victoria, huddled in the corner shuddering!

"Victoria – what's happening. It can't possibly be Darryn playing, can it?"

## Chapter 2

As both parents ran into the room, they were aware of their small son joining them from behind.

"Why is everybody up so early?" he was mumbling. "What's going on?"

His parents and sister did not answer and, as he followed their gaze, he realised why. The piano was playing itself! Victoria seemed very frightened, she being the one who had first heard the music, and the first one downstairs. Mum reached out to pull her close. Mum herself was quite shaken by what she saw and, as the whole family looked on, the piano continued to play, changing tempo, getting faster and faster, louder and louder, making a great thumping sound which threatened to wake the whole neighbourhood. The beautiful strains of music they had heard from upstairs now seemed angry and frenzied, and the family could do nothing but wait until the piano eventually fell silent.

The family too were silent, shocked and stunned by what they had just witnessed. Victoria was visibly shaking, and her mother had turned a ghastly shade of white. Dad was the first to speak.

"Well, what on Earth was all that about?" he said, sitting down on the nearest chair and pulling Darryn onto his knee.

"Oh no, I didn't want it to stop!" said Darryn. "That was great fun!"

"Great fun?" echoed Victoria. "Don't be so stupid. It was terrifying! How did it manage to play its own keys – no-one was touching it. It's not one of those wind-up ones, is it, Mum? You know, the kind you turn the key and the piano plays certain tunes?" She looked at her Mum hopefully.

"I don't think so," replied Mum and, though before she had been pretty sure this wasn't the case, she decided to go and have another look. She and Victoria checked eve-where they could think of – underneath, on top, at the back, even looking at the pedals for any clues as to what might have just taken place.

"Nothing there, I'm afraid," said Mum, finally giving up.

The family sat around in silence, each with their own thoughts.

"No wonder it was such a bargain," Dad was thinking to himself. "It must be haunted or something." As the thought entered his head, he dismissed it just as quickly, reminding himself he didn't believe in ghosts!

The ringing of the front door bell shook them again. Darryn jumped up from Dad's knee and ran towards the front door to see who was there. It was Simon from two doors along.

"Hey, Darryn, didn't know if you were back or not. Are you going back to school today?"

Dad looked at his watch. 10 minutes before 8 am. Kids! What on earth was Simon doing at the front door over an hour before school went in!

Victoria reluctantly got to her feet.

"Suppose I'd better start getting ready for school, too. What a strange start to the day," she yawned as she started to climb the stairs.

Mum and Dad looked at each other.

"Well, do you have any explanation?" Mum asked. Dad looked thoughtfully at the piano.

"Trick of the light? We imagined the whole thing? Who on earth knows? Let's go get some breakfast, I think better on a full stomach."

# Chapter 3

Mum replaced the telephone on the receiver and sat down with a sigh.

"What's wrong dear?" asked Dad, looking up from his newspaper.

"Auntie Maud has died. That was the matron of the nursing home on the telephone."

"I didn't know Auntie Maud was sick," said Darryn, between mouthfuls of breakfast cereal.

"She wasn't really sick, darling, just old, and tired too, I suppose. She was 93 you know." She turned towards Dad. "The funeral's tomorrow. The matron was unable to reach me, obviously, since we were on holiday. I know you won't be able to make it, but I'll go. There won't be many there, I shouldn't think, and anyway I'd like to pay my respects. I know we weren't close but, still, she was family." She smiled at the children. "Come on, you two, hurry up and finish breakfast, or you'll be late for school. And remember, Victoria, piano lessons straight after school. Your first exam must be coming up soon, isn't it?"

"Yes," replied her daughter. "Next week, actually. I'm not worried, though. Miss Stewart says that if I can play *Fleur de Lys* for my exam as well as I play it in practice I'll pass no problem."

"Don't get too complacent, young lady." said Dad, folding his newspaper and draining the contents of his cup. "You can never practice too much."

Turning to kiss his wife goodbye, he did not see his daughter raise her eyes to heaven then stick her tongue out in the direction of her younger brother, who sat watching her. Victoria jumped down from the table, grabbed her schoolbag and made for the door.

"Catch you later," she shouted over her shoulder. She blew Darryn a kiss. "Bye, darling," she mimicked Mum, and ran out of the door before Darryn could take aim with his spoon.

"Ugh! Sisters!" he exclaimed. "I'll get her back tonight," he thought, and ate the rest of his breakfast as he decided what substance he could use to gunge her with when she got home.

After Dad had gone, Mum cleared away the breakfast dishes while Darryn sneaked a look at what she had put in his schoolbag for his morning play snack. and thought about the story he was going to tell Simon.

"10 minutes to 9," Mum said, looking at the clock. "Better go."

Darryn was still regarded as being too little to walk to school on his own so Mum drove him there and picked him up in the afternoons.

"Next year, maybe," he thought, looking enviously at some older boys walking on their own.

Mum had a busy day, catching up with all the holiday washing and ironing and getting the house in order. She looked around the rooms fondly.

She wasn't sure that she wanted to move house, though Dad seemed to have his heart firmly set on buying the old house at the top of the hill. They had gone to see it just before setting off on holiday and, though Mum admitted there was a certain charm about the old place, she just didn't know if she was ready to leave her home. The children had always lived here, their friends were here, and both their schools were of a good standard and within walking distance.

"They'll meet new friends when we move," Dad had said, "and maybe they can still go to the same schools – there are buses they can catch after all."

Mum sighed. The new house was beautiful, she supposed, and the garden was much bigger than the one they had just now.

The old gentleman who lived there had had a conservatory built onto the house only a few years previously. Wheelchair-bound, this was where he spent his days looking out over his beloved garden. Mum and Dad had both agreed that this room, full of sunlight, would be perfect for use as the children's playroom. The old man's daughter had only recently persuaded him to go and live with her, and so the house had been put up for sale. Dad had been so excited.

"It's within our price range, dear," he had

said when Mum had expressed doubt, and she still felt the same niggling doubt.

She seemed unable to shake the feeling as she went from room to room, picking up discarded items of clothing from Victoria's bedroom, and rescuing suspended "bungee-jumping" dolls from inside Darryn's window. Smoothing out the little doll's dress, she put her back in Victoria's bedroom making a mental note to tell Darryn that, while bungee jumping was all right for his toy soldiers, it wasn't really suitable for his sister's elegant fashion dolls.

Going into the children's playroom, Mum ran her duster over the piano keys. The notes sounded as she touched them, but there was no repeat performance of the tune-playing which had taken place earlier. Perhaps they had imagined it, Mum thought to herself, as she polished the top of the piano.

"After all, how can a piano play on its

own? We were all probably over-tired from the long drive back from holiday."

She closed the lid, pushed in the piano stool and left the room.

"Now," she thought, "is my black suit in a fit state to be worn to the funeral?"

Shaking out the duster, she climbed the stairs to her bedroom to examine the contents of her wardrobe.

# Chapter 4

"Good, Victoria. That was quite good," nodded Miss Stewart as her young pupil finished playing. "Now, do you want to slot in another practice before your exam next Tuesday?"

"It's good of you to ask, Miss Stewart," the young girl smiled as she got up, "but my Mum and Dad just bought a new piano, so now I'll be able to practice any time I want."

"Did they really, dear? Well isn't that just marvellous. I do hope you put it to good use,

Victoria. You have talent, you know, but you must remember the key word . . ."

"*Discipline*," thought Victoria.

". . . discipline," said Miss Stewart, right on cue. "You must discipline yourself if you want to be a really good pianist."

Victoria, her back toward her teacher, mouthed the words in perfect timing with Miss Stewart. Though she was a good teacher, and Victoria did like her, her use of the word discip*line* could be a bit wearing at times. Folding her music sheets and placing them inside her folder, Victoria nodded as Miss Stewart droned on and on.

"I had a pupil once, way before your time, who could have made something of herself. Extremely talented she was, and a real pleasure to teach. Then she lost interest, you see, as she progressed. She found it was becoming more like hard work than pleasure, and she simply didn't have the discipline to see it through."

Victoria stared hard at her training shoes. Honestly, if she had to listen to this story once more, she thought she'd scream. Next she'd get the bit about getting interested in boys, and not bothering to turn up for lessons.

"Of course, the next thing you know, she's not bothering to turn up for lessons, choosing instead to 'hang out' at the burger bar, making eyes at the young men who frequented it."

Pointedly pulling up her sleeve to look at her watch, Victoria grabbed at her bag and turned towards the door.

"Miss Stewart, I'm sorry, I really don't mean to interrupt, but I have to go. I promised Mum I'd help her clear out the playroom tonight. Sorry, I'll see you next week, though."

"Oh, right, bye then dear."

From where she now sat on the sofa, Miss Stewart removed her glasses and rubbed her eyes.

"Half an hour till my next pupil," she observed, looking at the clock on the mantelpiece. "Think I'll just have a little snooze while I wait." And, placing her feet on the little stool before her, she pulled her cardigan around her shoulders and fell fast asleep.

Later that night, when dinner was over, and the last of the children's toys had been boxed in the playroom, Dad suggested that Victoria play *Fleur de Lys* for them.

Settling herself on the piano stool, Victoria began to play. At first she faltered a little, then, as she grew in confidence, the notes flowed perfectly from beneath her fingers.

Dad sat back in his chair and closed his eyes.

"Isn't that beautiful," he thought to himself, pleased after all that they had made the purchase of the piano.

Then, suddenly, the haunting melody

changed pace. The notes emanating from the piano became louder and faster and, as Dad opened his eyes and sat forward in his chair, he saw that his daughter was no longer playing the instrument but had recoiled back in fright, her fingers suspended in mid-air. Darryn was jumping up and down excitedly.

"It's doing it again, it's doing it again!" he screamed.

Mum was on her feet and making her way towards her daughter. She put her arm around the girl's shoulders and stared, entranced, at the keys.

The piano seemed to have a mind entirely of its own, and the family noticed after a while that it played the same tune over and over, only sometimes more quickly and, it seemed, more angrily than others. Eventually the playing stopped, and both parents turned to look at one another.

"Imagination? Trick of the light?" said

Mum. "I don't think so, somehow. There's something strange happening here, and we have to find out what it is."

# Chapter 5

Mum shook hands with the rosy-cheeked woman standing before her.

"She was a lovely old soul, really she was. Gave a lot of pleasure to a lot of people, she did. She loved to sing, and always did a little spot at the monthly concerts we had in the home."

Mum smiled at the matron.

"Yes," she agreed, "I remember her singing. When I was much younger my father used to take me to visit Auntie Maud and sometimes she would sing – only because he asked her, of course, for as you'll know she wasn't one to brag about things."

The two spoke fondly of the old lady then, when they heard the organist begin to play inside the little chapel attached to the crematorium, they made their way inside.

"I was right about the amount of people attending," thought Mum as she pulled off her gloves and took a seat.

Apart from herself, the matron and the chaplain, there were only three other people in the chapel. It wasn't that Maud hadn't been liked, she thought to herself, it was just that all the friends she'd had were either dead or too frail and infirm to attend the service.

There was a hymn first, then the chaplain said a few words about Maud and the kind of person she'd been. When he'd finished speaking, the organist started to play as the coffin moved out of sight behind the black velvet drapes.

"But that's the same tune!" thought Mum disbelievingly. "It's exactly the same tune as the one the piano's been playing at home!" She glanced at the organist, but her face was impassive as she played each note.

Looking down at the order of oervice which had been given to her when she entered the chapel, she picked it up and scanned it quickly.

Hymn:       The Lord's My
            Shepherd
Blessing:   Father Christopher
            Blount
Organ Solo: The Ancient Oak, by
            Jessica Perry

She stopped reading. Jessica Perry – she knew that name. It had seemed familiar straight away, but from where did she know it?

People were standing, she noticed, as the final hymn was being sung. She pushed the order of service into her bag and joined the others in song.

It wasn't until she was stopped at traffic lights on the way home that she remembered. Of course, Jessica Perry. *Nurse* Jessica Perry. She had been the midwife who had helped deliver Victoria over 12 years ago, *and* she was a piano teacher too.

Emily Houston remembered her well. Almost the same age as herself, Nurse Perry had been with her throughout what had been a particularly difficult birth, and seemed to take almost as much delight in the newly-born, red-faced screaming child as the proud parents themselves did. She had visited mother and daughter every day for each of the eight days they spent in hospital – Mum having developed a throat infection and baby Victoria a bad case of jaundice.

Shaken from her reverie by the sound of a car horn sounding behind her, Mum noticed the lights had changed to green, pushed the gear stick into first gear and moved off. She didn't know Jessica had had any music published, but then why should she? They had lost touch over eight years ago when Jessica had transferred to another hospital and left the district. Mum wondered if she had ever married. She knew Jessica had been keen to have children of her own, and that she had been very fond of Victoria, visiting whenever she could and *never* forgetting a birthday. Indeed, it had been Jessica who had given the little girl her first piano, when she was only 3 years old. It was a little pink one, with animal stickers on either side, and each key had a corresponding letter of the alphabet painted just above it. Using the little book which accompanied the piano, Mum had helped Victoria to play the tunes which were "spelt out" in the book, until gradually Victoria could play by herself.

Arriving home, Mum parked the car in the driveway and went inside.

Dad and the two children sat around the kitchen table, and Mum knew by the almost audible sound of silence that there was something wrong.

"How did it go, love?" asked Dad as Mum took off her coat and put down the car keys.

"Okay," she replied, pulling up a chair. "But what's wrong with you lot? You look as if you are in a state of shock."

"It's the piano, Mum," blurted out Darryn, who could barely contain himself. "This time it played for me. I was just practising my scales . . ."

Dad frowned in Darryn's direction.

"You were what?" he prompted.

"Well, I was about to practice my scales," he corrected. I was trying to hold down as many black notes as I could with one hand, and making my feet reach the pedals at the same time, when it started again!."

"What did?" asked Mum.

Dad cleared his throat.

"The piano started playing itself again, Emily. Just as it's done previously, repeating the notes over and over."

"The same tune?" asked Mum.

"No, not this time," replied Dad. Trying to smile, he said "I think it's trying to show us it has more than one tune in its repertoire."

Mum glanced at Victoria.

"Are you all right?" she asked, taking hold of her daughter's hand.

"Yes, I'm all right, Mum, thanks. I was frightened before when I thought it was only me that caused the piano to play, but today it was Darryn who was playing when the piano completely took control. I'm really curious now, though. I'd love to know what's really going on."

Mum took the order of service from her handbag and placed it on the kitchen table.

"Okay," she said, "here's the story so far."

And she told them what she knew about Nurse Jessica Perry.

"I remember her, of course, I do," said Dad. "But what does all this mean? Do you think it was her piano that we bought? A haunted piano which plays only her tunes?"

Looking at her young son's face, eyes widening at every word his father said, Mum shook her head in Dad's direction.

"Of course not." she said. "I mean, you have to be dead before you can haunt things or people, don't you, and as far as I know Jessica's alive and well and living a few hundred miles away."

Almost to herself, she added quietly: "Though it would explain why I haven't had a card or a letter from her in years."

Then, realising all eyes were upon her, she shook herself and gave a little laugh.

"Oh come on you lot, don't look so serious. I don't mean to frighten you. It probably has nothing to do with Nurse Perry at all."

"We're not frightened, Mum," said Darryn, bravely. Though in all truth, words like "dead" and "haunted" were two of his least favourites. He wondered if he could sleep in Victoria's room tonight without her being aware of it!

"Right," said Dad, getting up to open the oven door. "Dinner should be almost . . . oh no!"

"What is it?" asked Mum, turning towards her husband.

"I am afraid the meatloaf you asked me to cook is just a bit, em, overdone." The meatloaf he removed from the oven was black and barely recognisable.

"But I wrote down 'cook for 1 hour at no. 3'" said Mum.

"Ah, that was a 3 was it?" He put the burnt offering in the dustbin before adding, "I thought it was an 8."

Opening the kitchen drawer, Mum pulled out a menu.

"Okay, guys, who wants pizza?"

# Chapter 6

Squinting at her alarm clock, Victoria saw it was 1 o'clock in the morning and wondered what had wakened her. Then, she realised she was not alone in the bed.

"Darryn!" she thought, looking at his sleeping face. "When did he appear?" And didn't he look angelic when he was asleep!

She lay back down and closed her eyes, but sleep eluded her. She tossed and turned, and plumped up her pillow, but all to no avail. She finally decided she was thirsty, and got out of bed. She donned her slippers and dressing gown and crept quietly along the hallway to the stairs.

"Victoria," she heard as she reached the second stair. She froze.

"Surely the piano can't talk as well!" she thought. Her heart pounded in her chest. Then, slowly lifting her slippered foot to continue her descent, she heard the voice again.

"Victoria!"

This time, though, she recognised the voice as belonging to her brother, and she turned to see him peering at her in the dark.

"Ssh," she put her fingers to her lips, then extended her hand upwards and motioned for him to come towards her.

The two children crept quietly down the stairs hand in hand and made their way into the kitchen. Seated at the table with glasses of milk and plates of cookies, the children kept their voices low as they spoke.

"Can't we put the light on?" Darryn asked his sister.

## Chapter 6

"No," she replied. "We don't want to wake Mum and Dad. The moon's really bright tonight, anyway, we don't need the light on."

"Why, and when for that matter, did you come into my bed?" asked Victoria. "And stop doing that!"

Darryn stopped picking the chocolate chips out of his cookie and took a large gulp of milk.

"No reason," he lied. "I just felt a bit cold, that was all."

"Cold?" said Victoria scornfully. "In the middle of the one of the warmest springs we've ever known, you were cold? Tell the truth, Darryn, you were afraid, weren't you?"

"Afraid? Afraid of what?" he stammered. "I'm not afraid, Victoria, I told you, I was just cold."

"All right, Darryn," his sister relented, reminding herself that he was only 6 years old and that she herself had been scared out of her wits the first time the piano had played. "Look, if I admit to being just a teensy bit scared, you can admit to it too. I promise I won't tell Simon. Anyway, betcha if this happened in his house he'd be blubbering like a baby, he'd be so afraid."

The thought of Simon, his dearest friend, who always had to play the part of the hero no matter what game they played, blubbering like a baby, cheered Darryn considerably.

As quickly as he had smiled, though, a worried frown spread across his face.

"Victoria," he began.

"Mmm?"

"Would you think I was being really stupid if I suggested something about the piano?"

"No, of course I wouldn't." Victoria looked up from her empty plate. "What is it?"

"Well," Darryn began slowly, "you know this Nurse Jessica person Mum was talking about, and how the piano keeps playing her tunes?"

"Well, we know one of the tunes is hers, yes" agreed Victoria.

"Well, do you think it's possible . . . that, maybe . . ."

"Darryn, spit it out!" his sister began to lose patience. "Come on, I want to go back to bed, so hurry up and say what you're thinking."

"Promise you won't laugh?"

Sighing, Victoria lifted her glass and plate from the table and made towards the sink.

"I'm going to bed," she said.

"Okay, okay, I'll say it," said Darryn. His sister sat back down. "I think someone murdered Nurse Perry, put her body inside the piano, and her spirit is playing the tunes to let us know her body is in there," he said.

Victoria looked aghast.

"Murdered? Put her body inside? No wonder you couldn't sleep, Darryn, thinking such horrid thoughts."

"I knew you wouldn't believe me," her brother sighed.

"Well, let's face it, Darryn," she said, a little more gently this time, "it is a bit far fetched. But then, if you were to tell someone about a piano that played by itself, they would think that was far fetched, wouldn't they?"

The two children sat quietly for a while.

"Do you want to go and look?" ventured Victoria.

Darryn said nothing for a while, then, "I think we have to. I don't see how anyone can sleep properly in this house, when there may be a dead body inside our piano!"

# Chapter 7

The house was deathly silent as the two children crept along the hall. Just before they reached the playroom, Victoria trod on something sharp and had to stop herself from crying out.

"What's wrong?" asked Darryn.

His sister bent down and picked up a plastic dinosaur.

"That's what's wrong," she hissed at him. "When are you going to learn to pick up your toys?"

Shaking her head, she tucked the dinosaur under her arm, intending to throw it into one of the boxes in the playroom.

The two children entered the room.

"Did you bring Dad's torch?" asked Darryn.

Victoria nodded and indicated the flashlight in her left hand. The two children crept to the far end of the room where the piano stood.

"Okay," said Victoria, "we're not going to be able to see anything unless we stand on top of the stool." Pulling it towards her, trying to make as little noise as possible, she motioned to Darryn to climb up. "We'll both have to stand on it, then one of us can lift the lid and the other one can shine the torch to let us see inside."

Darryn moved towards the stool to do as his sister said. How he wished he'd kept his big mouth shut. He was afraid now. The playroom looked very different in the moonlight. Every toy box looked as though it hid something awful behind it, and he had jumped at the sight of a huge being reflected on the wall. Looking down, he realised it was one of his action figures, the one which had a yellow and green skull instead of a face, and bright red glowing coals where there should have been eyes. Funny how it looked so menacing when magnified to six times its normal size!

His heart pounding, he stepped on top of the stool. Suddenly, there was a tapping noise at the window.

"What was that?" he grabbed at his sister, almost knocking both himself and her off their unsteady perch.

"It's only the wind," she whispered, turning towards the window. He saw that the window was open and that the curtain blew, causing the venetian blinds to rattle against the window pane. He steadied himself again and took the torch his sister held out towards him.

"Ready?" she asked.

He nodded uncertainly. "What if there is a body in there?" he thought to himself. "What then?"

Victoria leant forward and made to lift the lid. This time the tapping noise was louder. Only now it was more a sort of scuffling noise. She glanced back at her brother.

"Did you hear that?" she whispered.

Did he hear it?! He was petrified! It hadn't been the wind at all! It was the body inside the piano, he knew it was, scratching helplessly at its wooden grave, trying to get out! He'd known it all along!

In his haste to get down from the stool he dropped the torch and, trying to catch it before it hit the ground, completely lost his balance and grabbed onto his sister's leg trying to save himself. Victoria tried to keep a hold on the piano to stop herself from falling, but the partially lifted lid slammed shut on her fingers, causing her to emit a blood curdling scream.

Minutes later, Dad threw open the playroom door and switched on the light. He could not believe the sight which greeted him. Victoria, tears sliding down her face, knelt on the floor nursing her rapidly swelling fingers. Her brother, meanwhile, lay not far from her with his leg twisted uncomfortably beneath him.

"What on earth is going on?" he asked, aware that he seemed to have been asking that question just a bit too often recently.

Victoria tried to speak, sobs choking her.

"Oh Dad, we're sorry, we were just trying to see inside the piano – we didn't want to wake you up, but we've made such a mess of things now. My poor fingers," she wept, "I think I've broken them!"

Mum had by now joined them in the playroom and was helping Darryn to sit up.

"Are you all right? Do you think you can stand?" she asked her son, who was also in tears.!

"I've probably broken it in five places!" he wailed.

"Hush now," his mother chided. "Hold my hands and try to stand, there's a good boy."

Tentatively, and clinging tightly to his Mum, the young boy moved to a standing position.

"Ow, it hurts, Mum, it really hurts!"

"Okay, dear, I know, but just keep a tight hold of me and try taking a couple of steps." Mrs Houston could tell that, although Darryn had undoubtedly hurt himself, his leg was not broken. "Thank Heavens for that," she said to herself.

Dad, meanwhile, was shaking his head as he looked at his daughter's fingers.

"Victoria, Victoria, whatever shall we do with you?" He held her hands gently. "Come on, dry your tears, and tell me what this was all about."

Through muffled sobs, Victoria related the story to her disbelieving father.

"And then there was a scuffling noise, and Darryn dropped the torch and . . ." She stopped and turned towards the piano. "Listen, there it is again."

The whole family listened. And, sure enough, a strange noise did seem to come from the corner in which the piano stood. Darryn moved closer to his Mum, involuntarily tightening his grip on her fingers.

"See" he almost accused his sister. "I told you it wasn't the wind. There *is* something inside the piano!"

As Dad stood up and went to take a closer look, the sound came again, but this time from behind the piano rather than in it.

"Give me a hand, love," he said to his

wife and, between them, they pushed one end of the piano out from the wall.

"There's your dead body," he grinned. A little starling lay in the corner of the room.

"It's only a baby," said Mum. "There's a nest of them outside our bedroom window. It must have flown in through this open window and the poor little thing's not been able to find its way back out."

Sore leg almost completely forgotten, Darryn joined his parents looking at the poor little bird.

"Is it hurt?" he asked.

"I don't think so, son" replied his Dad. "Just a bit shaken and probably more than a little scared. I'll try and pick him up so he can get back to the nest."

The little bird, not yet having the sense to know he could simply flap his wings and fly off, hopped about the floor in fear when he saw the huge giant approach him. Dad eventually managed to lift the little bird and, after checking there was nothing wrong with it, opened the window wide and set it outside on the window ledge.

"There, he'll be just fine now. He'll go back to his family, none the worse for wear, I shouldn't think."

He turned back to see Mum gently rubbing Victoria's fingers.

"Dead bodies, indeed," she gently chastised her. "And you have your exam next week too – just as well your fingers aren't broken – we'll have to hope the swelling goes down quite quickly."

Victoria sighed and nodded her head in agreement.

"It was pretty stupid, I suppose. I mean we *could* have waited till morning, couldn't we?" She looked at her brother who was examining his leg for bruises, cuts and anything else he could boast of to Simon.

"I don't know if I'll be able to go to school tomorrow," he announced.

"Yes, well, we'll see about that in the morning," smiled Mum, greatly relieved that no-one seemed to have suffered more than surface bruising and injured pride. Hugging both her children, she turned them in the direction of the door and sent them upstairs to bed.

"Go on, now, off to bed, or we'll all oversleep tomorrow."

"All right, Mum, Dad, goodnight," they chorused and walked wearily upstairs.

"What a night!" she turned to her husband. "Dead bodies in pianos, I mean it's just too ridiculous for words." She yawned sleepily. "Come on, let's go to bed, I'm exhausted."

Dad nodded. "Yes, just coming dear."

Mum left the room but, as she put her foot on the third stair, she realised Dad wasn't following. She went back downstairs and pushed open the playroom door.

"Roger . . ." she began, then stopped as

## Chapter 7

she realised her husband was shining the torch inside the piano.

Looking up, he grinned sheepishly. "Just checking," he said.

# Chapter 8

Next morning everyone sat sleepily around the breakfast table.

"I'm so tired," said Victoria. "I must only have had about four hours sleep."

"I know, dear," her mother smiled. "We all feel the same way. We can have an early night tonight, after we get back from 'Treetops'."

"What's 'Treetops'?" asked Darryn, looking curiously at Mum.

"It's a house your father and I have been to look at, and we'd like you children to

come see it, too, before we decide on anything."

"Decide what?" asked Victoria, looking
from one to the other.

"Whether to buy it or not," said Dad. It's
a beautiful house, I know you're both going
to like it. We're very lucky to be given the
opportunity to buy it."

Victoria stopped eating.

"Buy another house? What – leave our
home? Why? When? I don't want to leave
here. Mum?" she turned towards her
mother. "Do you want to do this too?" she
asked. "I thought you loved it here?"

Mum looked at Dad anxiously then back
towards Victoria.

"It *is* a lovely house, dear," she said
reassuringly, "and the garden's huge – wait
till you see it."

Victoria pushed her plate away from her.

"I don't want to move house," she said
sulkily. "I want to stay here."

Darryn reached over to his sister's plate.

"Aren't you going to eat your bacon?" he asked, already lifting the food to his mouth.

Victoria looked disgustedly at him.

"You're so gross sometimes," she said. "Don't you even care about what's just been said."

"Course I care," he said. "It's just that I'm . . .hey, what did you do that for?" he turned angrily towards Victoria, who had clamped her hand over his mouth and was staring wide-eyed at the kitchen door.

"Ssh," she told him. "Be quiet – listen."

Everyone was still, and could hear, quite plainly, the sound of the piano playing loudly and angrily.

"Not again!" Dad shook his head and got to his feet.

Mum and the two children followed and made their way to the playroom. Dad opened the door and, once more, the family watched the piano and listened to the now familiar tune.

The piano thumped and banged, the vibrations causing the instrument to move slightly along the floor. The children stayed close to their parents, afraid of the angry sounds and air of tension which filled the room. Eventually, the piano seemed to tire and, though it continued to play, it was quieter now and the children became less afraid.

"Will you be all right in the house by yourself?" asked Dad.

"Of course I will," replied Mum. "Don't worry about me. You get off to work and I'll drop the children at school. I'll be just fine – what possible harm can a piano do to me?"

"If you're sure then, it's just that everything's so weird just now." He looked at his watch. "I really have to go, but I'll pick you all up at 6 pm tonight and we can drive over to 'Treetops'."

## Chapter 8

As though reacting to some sort of signal, the piano once more burst into angry banging and thumping, almost as though at the mention of the name of the new house.

"Wow!" said Darryn. "It's getting mad again!"

Dad pulled the door shut and led his family away from the noise. As they went back into the kitchen, Mum looked thoughtful.

"I'm going to call Jessica today," she said. "I don't know if she'll be of any help or not, but it's got to be worth a try, hasn't it?"

"But you have no idea where she lives," said her husband.

"No," she replied, "but I do know where she works. I'll ring the hospital."

# Chapter 9

When Dad arrived home that night just after 6 pm, Mum and the two children were waiting. They got into the car, Victoria looking desperately unhappy, and drove off in the direction of the large house.

"How was your day?" Mum asked Dad distractedly.

"Fine," he replied. "But how was yours? Any luck contacting Jessica?"

His wife sighed. Reluctant though she was to upset the children, they knew so much already there was little point in trying to hide anything from them.

"I rang the hospital this morning," she said, "and asked if I could speak to Nurse Jessica Perry. The young girl asked who I was then put me through to the matron. She's dead, Roger, *Jessica's dead*!" Mum bit her lip and looked down at her hands. "Over eight years ago, not long after she moved, apparently. I feel so awful, you know, no wonder I didn't hear from her – poor Jessica."

Arriving at the foot of the hill which would take the family on up to 'Treetops', Dad parked the car and switched off the engine.

"What happened?" he asked his wife quietly.

"A car accident," she said slowly. "A freak car accident when a lorry went out of control and ran straight into her. She was killed instantly – apparently she didn't suffer, so I suppose that's a blessing."

Her husband shook his head.

"That's awful, Emily. I'm so sorry."

"I know, such a tragic waste," Mum agreed. "She was on her way to her publishers, according to what the matron said. She'd confided her musical ambitions to her only the day before. Seemingly she had just completed a new piece of music and was taking it to her publishers on her day off to see what he thought of it. So I rang him, too, the publisher. Matron could only remember part of the firm's name, but I found them in the telephone book. I said I'd recently heard *The Ancient Oak* and wondered if Jessica Perry had written anything else. He was most helpful, the young man I spoke to, and was able to tell me she'd had one other piece of work published, *La Niña Hermosa*. Apparently it's Spanish for *The Beautiful Child* – her mother was of Spanish origin" she added, by way of explanation.

She paused for a moment, glancing in the

mirror at her two children. Both were listening intently, waiting to hear what she would say next. She cleared her throat.

"So, anyway, I've asked them to send copies of the two pieces of music to me. I think I'm fairly sure by now the one the piano plays most often, and most angrily, is *The Ancient Oak*, and I'd say it's a fair bet that *La Niña Hermosa* will be the other. Anyway, let's just wait and see, shall we?" She forced a smile. "Okay, everyone? Now come on, you too, don't look so glum. We'll get to the bottom of this mystery soon, and life will go back to being dull and boring again!"

Darryn had unconsciously moved closer to his sister in the back seat, and was now holding her hand.

"Ow, Darryn, not so tight," she yelped. "My fingers are still tender from the piano slamming incident – which incidentally was your fault!"

Darryn removed his hand indignantly.

"Sorry," he mumbled, "I forgot."

Dad turned the key in the ignition and moved away from the side of the road.

"Let's just wait till the music sheets arrive and we'll see if they are one and the same tunes, then we can take it from there."

A few minutes later, they arrived outside the house. The old gentleman, seated in his conservatory as usual, raised his hand in greeting. Darryn slammed shut the door of the car and gazed in wonder.

"But the garden's enormous, Dad. We can play football and basketball. Simon would never find me here in a game of hide and seek. Wow – when are we moving in?"

Victoria looked at him.

"Traitor," she said. "Have you no loyalty to your home – are you so flippant that you'd just up and move so you could play hide and seek?" She tutted and folded her arms crossly.

Mrs Houston put her hand gently on her daughter's shoulders.

"Come on, everyone, let's go inside. And don't be so hard on your brother, Victoria, he *is* only 6, remember?"

Mum and Victoria walked in the direction of the front door, with Dad following closely behind.

"Da-ad," shouted Darryn, running to keep up. "What does flippant mean?"

Even Victoria, sulky and unhappy, had to admit the house was beautiful. The old gentleman was charming and had instructed the family to feel free to explore every room. Though he was obviously unable to accompany them, he told them to store up any questions and he'd answer them later. Over tea and cake, served by the old man's daughter, he talked fondly of his home, and knowledgeably of its history. Though she had been determined not to, Victoria felt herself drawn to old Mr

Lawrence and to his house. Darryn was on the point of reaching out for his fourth cake when a look from his father caused him to withdraw his hand and sit back in his seat.

"So?" began Mrs Williams, Mr Lawrence's daughter. "What do you think?"

"Oh, we're very impressed," answered Mum. "It's a lovely house – you must have loved living here as a child."

"Yes, indeed," Mrs Williams smiled. "I have lots of happy memories, I have to say, but you can't live in the past forever. There comes a time when you simply have to move on, isn't that right, Dad?"

Mr Lawrence turned back from the window to look at his daughter. His wife had died almost 10 years ago now and he knew he couldn't realistically expect to stay in this house for much longer. Elizabeth, his daughter, had been very good to him over the years and he knew it made sense for him to go and live with her and her husband in their modern semi-detached house in town.

"Yes, dear, you're right, we all have to move on at some time in our lives." He hastily wiped away a tear before anyone could see it and managed a little smile. He liked this family, and he didn't mind the thought too much of them living in his precious home.

"Bring the place to life again," he thought, "the sound of children running through the house." Adjusting the rug tucked over his legs, he leant forward in his wheelchair. "Now then, young man" he held out the plate towards Darryn. "What about that fourth cake?"

Darryn and Victoria sat on the wooden bench outside the house while Mum and Dad said their goodbyes.

"We still have to put our own house on the market, you understand," Dad was saying. "But we are very interested in this one."

## Chapter 9

Mr Lawrence and his daughter nodded.

"I'd be very happy to see you and your family living here," the old man said. "I know when to accept gracious defeat," he smiled at his daughter, who reached for his hand.

"It was lovely to meet you all," she said to the family. "We hope to hear from you soon."

"We'll be in touch," said Dad, "and we do understand that if another buyer comes along you'll sell to him. After all, you can't wait for us forever!"

"I have a feeling we'll be doing business, young man," said Mr Lawrence as he made to turn his wheelchair and go back inside.

Victoria and Darryn got up to join their parents on the driveway. They waved to Mr Lawrence, who was by now back in the conservatory, and Darryn stopped and bent to pick up some acorns. Looking up, he had to shade his eyes from the sun.

"What an enormous tree," he observed, looking at the huge oak which stood to the left of the conservatory.

"Yeah," his sister agreed, "must have been here for centuries! Come on, let's get into the car, Mum and Dad are waiting."

# Chapter 10

The swelling had disappeared on Victoria's fingers after a couple of days and she resumed her position on the stool practising the piano. The music Mum had asked to be sent from the publishers did not arrive until three days later, during which time the piano burst into life on more than a few occasions. Sometimes it played gently, almost soothingly, but at others the whole playroom seemed to shake with its anger. Strangely, the morning the man called from the estate agents to take photographs of the house was one of the days the piano played at its loudest and most violent. When he began to hammer the "For Sale" sign into the garden, the noise from the piano was almost deafening.

"My daughter's practising for an exam," Dad mumbled apologetically to the man. "A bit heavy-handed, I'm afraid."

The man looked at him oddly, or was it Dad's imagination, and left quite soon after. Of course, as soon as his car disappeared from sight, the furious playing stopped.

Though perhaps uneasily, the family became used to the music filling the house, and tried not to let it disrupt their lives too much. Mum was the first downstairs each morning, checking the post, for she felt somehow that the clue to what this was all about was contained in those music sheets. When at last a large brown envelope was pushed through the letter box, Mum was almost afraid to open it. Victoria spotted it propped against the toaster when she came downstairs for breakfast.

"Is that it, Mum, is that the music?" she asked.

"I think so, love. I feel a bit uneasy about opening it."

"Then I'll do it," said her daughter. Victoria tore open the envelope and looked at the enclosed papers. "It's them, all right, Mum. *The Ancient Oak* and *La Niña Hermosa*." Victoria stared hard at *The Ancient Oak*. "It's definitely the same tune," she told her mother as she read the notes. "I've heard it so many times now I think I could write the notes down myself."

"Come on, Mum, let's go into the playroom. I want to try playing these for myself."

The two made their way to the playroom and Victoria took her place on the stool. Almost afraid, without really knowing why, Mum stood beside her daughter and watched her play. And Victoria played as though she herself had written both tunes. There was no hesitancy, whatsoever, only a comfortable familiarity which lent a delightful flow to the music. When she had finished, she turned towards her mother and gave a sad smile. Her eyes had filled with tears.

"She must have been a beautiful person, Mum, to be able to write such beautiful music." Mum smiled in agreement just as the door creaked open and Dad and Darryn stepped inside.

"We weren't sure if it was the piano or you," said Dad wryly. "Then when neither of you were in the kitchen we realised it must be you."

Seeing his daughter's tear-filled eyes he looked questioningly at his wife.

"Jessica's music arrived, then?" he asked.

"Yes, this morning. It's very beautiful, if you just remember to play it at the right tempo! Come on Victoria, let's leave the music for now," she gently pulled her daughter to her feet. "Go and have a shower, dear, and get ready for school. We can look at the music again later."

Victoria left the room, followed by her parents.

"Come on, Darryn, you too," said Dad.

"Coming," replied Darryn. "I've just spotted a toy I lost months ago." As he walked past the piano to reach the toy box, he could see that the keys of the piano shone and glistened rather more than usual. Curious, he picked up his toy and went to look at the piano more closely. He touched the keys tentatively, and was amazed to find that his fingers came away wet! Jumping back, he decided to get out of the room fast. As he closed the door behind him, he shrugged.

"If I didn't know any better," he thought, I'd swear the piano had been crying!"

# Chapter 11

"Victoria, where are you?" shouted Mum from the hallway.

"Up here Mum," her daughter replied. "In my bedroom." Victoria appeared at the top of the stairs and hung her head over the banister.

"Come down a minute, will you pet? I'm just going out and I need to speak to you first."

Victoria came downstairs and followed her mother into the front porch.

"I'm going to the supermarket now – are

you *sure* you don't want to come?" Her daughter shook her head.

"No, neither does Darryn," said Mum. "Okay, then, what time is it now?" She checked her watch. "6 o'clock, right. I'll go now and I should be back for about 7.30. Dad's having to stay late for a meeting, but he should be home round about the same time as me. All right? Darryn's playing with Simon outside – I'll tell him not to go too far and to do what you tell him." She raised her eyebrows none too hopefully at this remark. "Now, where *are* my car keys?"

Mum's car had no sooner left the driveway than the telephone rang. Victoria answered – it was her father.

"Victoria, hi, let me speak to your Mum, please?"

"You've just missed her, Dad, she's gone to the supermarket."

"Has she?" There was silence for a moment. "Look, Victoria, it seems this meeting may go on longer than I had first thought, so I may not get home until nearer 8.30 pm."

"Okay, Dad, I'll let Mum know when she gets back."

"Thanks, love, sorry about this. Will you guys be okay?"

"Course we will," she took another mouthful of the cola she had taken from the fridge. "Mum will be home in just over an hour and we'll see you about 8.30. Don't worry, Dad, we'll be just fine."

After saying goodbye to her father, Victoria replaced the receiver and went into the front room. She looked out of the window to see Darryn was still playing in the garden, then glanced up to check if the window was open. The heat both inside and out of the house was unbelievable for this time of the year. The window *was* open, as were all the other windows in the house, but there still didn't seem to be any air. Finishing what was left of her drink, Victoria went back upstairs to finish her homework.

"Now, do we need breakfast cereal, or not?" Mrs Houston mumbled to herself in the supermarket. She picked up a box anyway and made her way to the check-out.

"It's got awfully dark outside," said one of the women in the queue. "It's practically an eclipse," she looked at the check-out girl.

The young girl continued to zap the goods coming towards her on the conveyor belt and nodded her head distractedly. Mrs Houston looked at the sky, though, and was shocked to see how dark it had grown since she had entered the shop. She checked her watch. 7.15 pm. She hoped Darryn had gone inside the house for she now feared that maybe a storm was brewing. There was certainly something in the air. She'd be home soon, anyway – it was her turn next.

The woman in front pulled out her cheque book, almost at the same time as the

# Chapter 11

bored check-out girl's till roll ran out. Mrs Houston sighed.

"Why do I always join the wrong queue, and why is it always when I'm in a rush?"

# Chapter 12

Darryn *had* come in – not because of the threatening storm – but because Simon had been called in by his mother and Darryn grew bored outside in the garden by himself. He walked upstairs to his sister's room and entered without knocking.

"How many times have I told you to knock?" she said, not moving from her position on the bed. She was lying face down, reading a library book and listening to a CD.

"Sorry," mumbled Darryn, though he

wasn't. He couldn't care less who came into h*is* bedroom, and certainly would never think of asking anyone to knock before entering.

"I'm hungry," he told his sister.

"So, what's new?" she asked, still not lifting her head. "Why don't you go and get a bag of crisps?"

"There aren't any," he replied. "Hope Mum brings some back from the supermarket."

"Actually," said Victoria, putting down her book, "I'm quite hungry too. Let's go see what we can put in the microwave!"

Downstairs in the kitchen, Victoria had to switch on the light.

"I can't believe it's got so dark so early," she said. "It's just after 7 o'clock." She looked out of the window at the sky. "I hope we're not going to have a thunder storm."

Darryn emerged from the depths of the freezer, a package in each hand.

"What do you want?" he asked. "Potato waffles or chicken bites?"

"I don't mind – you choose," shrugged his sister, who was helping herself to more cola. Really, it was so hot, they probably *were* heading for a thunder storm, she thought.

"Then we'll have both," said Darryn happily. "Here," and he handed her the packets. Victoria read the cooking instructions quickly, put the waffles under the grill and the chicken in the microwave.

The first crack of thunder took them both completely by surprise. Victoria was seated on top of one of the tall kitchen stools leaning against the breakfast bar, while Darryn stood beside the microwave, counting down the minutes as though he didn't trust the oven to do it on its own. Darryn turned quickly to face his sister.

"Oh no," she whispered. "Please – not a thunder storm."

The next crack sent her flying off the stool

and away from the window to stand beside her brother.

"It's okay, Sis, it's only a little storm, we'll be fine."

Victoria was, and always had been, terrified of thunder and lightening. She had spent many a night in her parents' bed when such storms had raged before. Darryn, on the other hand, was totally unafraid and loved to stand at the window watching the bolts of lightening flash across the sky. He turned his attention back to the microwave to see how much cooking time remained, when there was a huge clap of thunder and the house was plunged into darkness.

"Victoria," he grabbed for his sister's arm, missing completely and instead knocking the can of cola from her hand, causing it to hit the floor and let its contents spill out. His sister's face was illuminated by the lightening which streaked across the sky and, in fact the whole kitchen was lit up, though only for an instant. Victoria took hold of her brother's hand.

"It's all right, Darryn," she tried to sound reassuring, but her voice was far from steady as she continued. "Mum and Dad will be here soon – all we have to do is stay calm and, before we know it, the power will be back on."

"A power cut? Does that mean I can't have my chicken bites?" he asked. "I'm starving."

Not letting go of his hand, Victoria felt her way to the fridge and took from inside a huge bar of chocolate.

"Here," she offered the bar to her brother. "That should keep you going for a while."

Their eyes grew accustomed to the dark and the two now looked at one another.

"Shall we stay here, do you think?" asked Darryn, "or go upstairs?"

Victoria was about to answer when she

heard a loud slam from the front of the house.

"What was that?" She looked at Darryn.

"It'll be Mum!" he said excitedly. "Mu—" he tried to shout.

Victoria put her hand over his mouth.

"Ssh," she whispered urgently. "How do you know it's Mum – I didn't hear a car pulling up, did you?"

Pulling her hand away from his mouth, Darryn turned on her angrily.

"How do you expect to hear anything above the noise of the thunder?" he asked. "Of course it's Mum – who else would it be?"

"Come over this way, Darryn," she instructed. "Come with me. We'll get Dad's flashlight, then we'll go investigate."

After considerable fumbling in the drawer, Victoria triumphantly produced the flashlight and the two children left the kitchen hand in hand. It wasn't necessary to try to be quiet going along the hall, for the sound of the storm raged furiously all around them. At this stage, both children knew that it was not their mother who had come in through the front door, for they would have met her in the hall before now. Wanting desperately to stop and change direction to go back to the comparative safety of the kitchen. Victoria knew that she had to make sure the front door was firmly locked first. Tightening her grip on Darryn's hand, she continued to shine the torch in front of them, determinedly placing one foot in front of the other, until they reached the door of the front porch.

"I'm scared, Victoria," said Darryn, his voice almost inaudible over the sound of the storm. "I want Mum and Dad to come home."

Victoria bent down closer to her brother.

"I'm scared too," she said, "but we have to lock the front door, then we can go telephone Dad at the office and tell him what's happened. He'll be home in 15 minutes, maximum, I promise, in fact he'll probably meet Mum outside in the driveway!" Victoria sounded a lot braver than she felt, and wished more than anything else in the world that her parents were here with them now. As she straightened up from talking to Darryn, the door slammed again, only this time there was the added noise of something smashing on the floor. Victoria swallowed hard and started to move forward.

It was at that moment that the torch batteries went flat.

# Chapter 13

Plunged once again into complete darkness, the children fell into each other's arms and clung together. Victoria sank down onto the floor, pulling her brother with her. Darryn was crying now, and Victoria was trying not to. As they sat there, the door repeatedly slammed open and shut, open and shut, thunder cracked and lightening flashed and now there was he added sound of something breaking and smashing onto the floor.

"I don't want to go any further, Victoria,

please. There must be someone in the porch, is there?" he looked up at his sister.

"I don't know if there's anyone there, Darryn, but I don't feel like going much further myself, especially without the torch."

The thunder had quietened to a rumble for now, and the children became aware of another noise. They listened intently.

"The piano!" said Victoria. "It's calling to us," she said, getting to her feet. "Come on," she told Darryn, "let's make our way to the playroom – the sound of the piano will guide us through the darkness and we can use the 'phone just outside the room to call Dad."

The frightened little boy got to his feet, clinging to his sister all the time. He didn't bother to question her instructions, he just wanted this whole nightmare to be over. Holding on to the wall, and to each other, the children returned along the route they

# Chapter 13

had just come, all the time aware of the slamming of the front door, interspersed with loud cracks of thunder. At the same time, though, the piano could be heard playing, as though beckoning to them to come to the playroom.

An extra loud bang of thunder was followed by a flash of lightening which momentarily lit up the house.

"Aargh!" wailed Darryn loudly, almost causing his sister to jump out of her skin.

"What now?" she asked, turning back to him.

"There," he pointed to a picture on the wall. Victoria squinted in the darkness. "It's the picture of you and I that Mum likes so much," she said. "What's so scary?"

"Phew," he breathed a sigh of relief. "Looked like some sort of alien creatures in the dark."

If she hadn't been so frightened, Victoria would have laughed. She thought the picture made them look like alien creatures in the daylight!

They had almost reached the door of the playroom, where the telephone was affixed to the wall. Victoria picked it up.

"How will you manage to see to dial the number? asked Darryn. Replacing the receiver she replied "No need to worry about that – it's dead. The 'phone lines must be down too."

They entered the playroom, where the piano still played.

"How strong do you feel?" Victoria asked her brother.

"Depends what for?" he looked at her curiously.

"I think we should wheel the piano over in front of the door so that no-one can get in." Then, seeing his ashen face, she added: "Until Mum and Dad get home, that is. As soon as we know it's them, we'll let them in – okay?"

## Chapter 13

Her brother looked doubtfully at the instrument in the corner.

"Do you think we can?" he asked.

"Of course," said Victoria with bravado. "Let's do it!"

And they did. While the storm outside still showed no sign of abating, the two children determinedly pushed and pulled at the piano until they had it positioned right against the playroom door.

"I feel safer now," said Victoria, smiling at her brother. He smiled back, reaching in his pocket for the half-melted chocolate bar.

"Let's sit over there on the bean bag and eat this," he said. "We can tell one another stories for a while."

The piano was quiet now and looked almost to be standing guard over them both. Every now and again, a flash of lightening would appear to light up the room, and the children would use this as an opportunity to retrieve something from the toy boxes. So far, Darryn had recovered a wooden bridge which had once been part of his train set, an (unbelievably) intact dinosaur jigsaw, a 5-coloured pen, and a multicoloured laser torch.

"A torch!" exclaimed Victoria, who had discovered her little pink piano from all those years ago, and was gently running her fingers over the keys. "Does it work?" she asked excitedly. Darryn moved the switch from "off" to "on", and the two were delighted to see a green light dance on the wall.

"Brilliant," said Victoria, clapping her hands. "Position it between us so we can both get the benefit, would you?"

Doing as he was bid, Darryn wedged the torch between the small wooden bridge and an old nursery rhyme book and went off to rummage in, what looked like from here, the "creepy crawly" toybox!

Victoria was still humming *The Ancient*

*Oak* since the piano had played it earlier, and was absentmindedly playing the notes on her pink piano. She looked at the keys as she hit each one, the letter 'D' corresponding with the first note she played. The second note read 'O' above it, the third 'N', then back to 'O' again. When she touched the fifth key, Victoria was beginning to realise this was not just a jumble of letters, instead it looked like the piano was trying to give her a message.

"Darryn," she called excitedly. "Darryn, come and see this. The tune means something – quickly." Darryn scrambled over towards his sister and watched. "Get the pen, quickly, write down each letter as I play the notes." She hummed out loud as she slowly picked out each note.

D O N O T

the little piano spelt.

Darryn looked at the letters he had written then moved closer to see what the rest of the message would be. Victoria played the next note, and the next, until the message was clear to them both:-

D O N O T B U Y T R E E T O P S

"Do not buy 'Treetops'!" Darryn repeated. "But why not? It doesn't make sense."

Victoria looked at the large piano standing on the other side of the room and wondered.

"Was this what it had been trying to tell them then, ever since it had come into their possession? A message from the grave conveyed through a piano?"

What Victoria would have dismissed a few months ago as being utter nonsense she now wasn't so quick to disregard.

"Victoria," Darryn insisted. "Why would the piano tell us not to buy a house – I don't understand."

His sister leant back against the bean bag.

"I don't understand either, Darryn. I'm

not sure that I ever will. Anyway," she pointed out to him, "there hasn't been any thunder for at least 10 minutes – maybe the storm's decided to move on."

The children cuddled up together, pulling a shawl over them that they had been wrapped in as babies and, to the sound of heavy rainfall outside, the two fell sound asleep.

# Chapter 14

"That's the telephone working again," said Dad as he picked up then replaced the receiver for the hundredth time that morning.

"That's good, dear," replied his wife. "Now all we need is for the electricity to go back on and we're in business."

The previous night Mr and Mrs Houston had, indeed, met one another outside the house. Mum's car had simply refused to start when she was ready to leave the supermarket, and she'd had to take shelter from the storm for some time before anyone was able to help her. Eventually a young man had kindly looked under her bonnet, affixed jump leads and got her moving. She set off, slowly, driving carefully back to her children.

Dad, meanwhile, coming late from his meeting, had been shocked to find that the nearer he got to home the greater number of houses seemed to have been affected by the storm. Most places were in complete darkness.

Pulling into the road almost at the same moment, both jumped from their cars and ran into the gloomy house. They had eventually, after deducing where the children must be, hammered and banged on the door of the playroom before they managed to wake them. Much hugging ensued, followed by Victoria showing her parents, by torchlight, the message she had uncovered earlier. Astounded, Mr and Mrs

Houston had made her repeat the tune slowly.

"She's right, you know," said Dad. "That's exactly what it says."

Mum nodded. "But why would Jessica not want us to buy another house?" she wondered aloud.

The four spent the night together in Mum and Dad's bedroom, rather crushed but safe and happy. Next morning, Dad repaired the front door which had broken one of its hinges the previous night. And two of Mum's pot plants lay shattered on the porch floor. Helping Dad to clear up, Darryn couldn't imagine what he and Victoria had been so afraid of last night. A door slamming and a porch full of geraniums and daffodils! So what! He'd tell Simon a totally different version of events, that was for sure!

Victoria and Mum were upstairs.

"I'm sure Jessica wrote *La Niña Hermosa* for you." Mum was saying. "She adored you, Victoria, especially since she never did have any children of her own."

"Emily," Dad shouted. "Come down quickly, there's something I must show you."

Mother and daughter quickly descended the stairs to see what all the commotion was about. Dad held out the morning newspaper towards his wife. She glanced at the page – most articles were concerned with the new Government which had just come into power – but her husband pointed towards a smallish feature on the bottom left hand corner.

"FREAK STORM TRAGEDY" the headline read.

"A freak thunderstorm wreaked havoc on the little town of Plessington last night. A large part of the neighbourhood was cut off from the electricity supply, with telephone lines also being affected. Tragically, Mr Jeremy Lawrence, late of

'Treetops', Mill Road, was killed when the large oak tree which stood beside his house was struck by lightning. The tree crashed through the conservatory, delivering a fatal blow to the old gentleman.

Mr Lawrence, whose family had lived in 'Treetops' for generations . . ."

Mum put down the paper on the hall table and leant against her husband to steady herself. Victoria grabbed the paper and began reading aloud.

"Oh no," she gasped. "Poor old Mr Lawrence. But don't you see, Mum, Dad, that's why Jessica was warning us not to go. She knew the accident was going to happen – it could have been us who were killed!"

Darryn was pulling at his mother's skirt.

"What is it dear?" she asked distractedly.

"This just came for you," he said, handing her a large brown envelope.

"What? Oh, right, thank you." Carelessly she tore it open, her thoughts still with Mr

Lawrence. As she pulled the letter from the envelope, she saw it was from the same publishers who had sent her the two pieces of music Jessica had written.

Dear Mrs Houston

<u>Miss Jessica Perry</u>

Your recent enquiry concerning the above caused us to search through files we had previously archived. Miss Perry's file contained a document addressed to a Miss Victoria Houston, however gave no address. In the hope that it may belong to your family, we are forwarding it to you. If, however, it has no relevance to you, please return it to us in the enclosed envelope.

Yours, etc . . .

Mum reached back inside the large envelope and pulled out a slimmer one, bearing Victoria's name. She handed it to her daughter.

"From Jessica," she said.

Victoria carefully opened the envelope and removed a sheet of music, entitled *La Guardián Angel*.

We hope you enjoyed this story from the Creepers series. There are six titles for you to collect:

This series was conceived by Edgar J Hyde and much of the text was provided by his minions under slavish conditions and pain of death! Thankfully none of the minions defied their master and so we can say 'thank you' to them for toughing it out and making this series possible

# Ghost Writer

Charlie is a 15-year-old, budding writer. When his family move to a large old house in the country he becomes the unsuspecting contact for a spirit writer who is trying to communicate with the living. How can the strange passages that appear overnight, in Charlie's own handwriting, be the work of anyone else but him? Who will believe his incredible story? The ghost seems to be trying to tell him of a dark secret and a cruel injustice. When Charlie starts to have a chilling recurring dream about his own death and he and his brother, Neil and sister, Kate start to see apparitions, they decide that they must investigate the ghost writer's secret – with terrifying consequences!

# Mirror Mirror

When she and her family visit a local antique shop to buy a fabulous mirror, Sophie is tranfixed by a music box ballerina and insists that she must have it. Little do any of the family know of the dark and tragic history behind the mirror and the music box, and their link to the person who calls herself the Keeper of Lost Souls. Sophie and her sisters, Amy-Beth and Lucy , with the help of their unpredictable Aunty Patsy, must discover the true story of the girl in the mirror. They must free her from the terrifying past that the mirror has witnessed and makes her relive again and again.

# The Piano

Roger and Emily Houston can't believe the bargain they have found when they buy a piano for a mere £200 – just perfect for the piano lessons of their children Victoria and Darryn. Their delight soon turns to amazement and horror – the piano has a life (or is that a death?) of it's own. The melodies that it plays over and over again are (literally) haunting and it becomes clear that someone from their past has a message for the Houston family about a very important decision they are about to make.

# The Scarecrow

A horrific attack takes place on an isolated farm. A shivering, terrified man is found in shock, his tongue removed. The shock is too much for him and he kills himself leaving a note which claims that he was a burglar who was stopped from breaking into the farm by a scarecrow, who then ripped out his tongue. Of course no-one believes the note. But, David, who lives on the farm, knows that the noisy farmyard cockerel has been found throttled, his beloved dog has mysteriously gone missing and Jonesy a harmless local character has also been viciously silenced – they must be connected with the sightings of a scruffy, barely-human creature on the prowl. David decides he must solve the mystery himself but doesn't realise just what he is getting himself into.

# The Wishing Well

Tom's family have moved to a farm in the country and he is very unhappy about the whole idea. To make matters worse his first day at his new school is as bad as he had at first dreaded and the imbecilic school bullies are soon after him. Tom finds sanctuary in a peaceful area of his family's new property that contains an old well. To his amazement and delight a heartfelt wish for revenge against his enemies spoken into the echoing depths of the well comes true. But Tom is about to find out that every malicious wish for revenge that is granted includes a sinister payback for the well's evil sprite occupant and soon the chaos she is creating seems uncontrollable. How can Tom stop her before she destroys everything and everyone in her path?

# Beggar Boy

Life isn't easy for Tommy and his mother. The most important things in life for the rest of the occupants of Montague Street are money and status symbols, and these are two things that Tommy and his mother definitely do not have. The shallow and cruel children of the street taunt Tommy by calling him 'beggar boy'. Just when he thinks he can stand no more of their petty jibes, a strange ragged boy comes to his defence. Tommy is appreciative but puzzled at the sudden appearance of his scruffy friend and at his new ally's amazing talent for creating fear and chaos in the lives of his affluent enemies. Where does the boy come from and, more puzzlingly, how can he appear and disappear so quickly?